numbers

Photography
George Siede and Donna Preis

Publications International, Ltd.

7373 North Cicero Ave.
Lincolnwood, Illinois 60712

3rd Floor, 3 Princes Street
London W1R 7RA

0-7853-7057-9

Publications International, Ltd.

1
one

1

one sock

2
two

two shoes

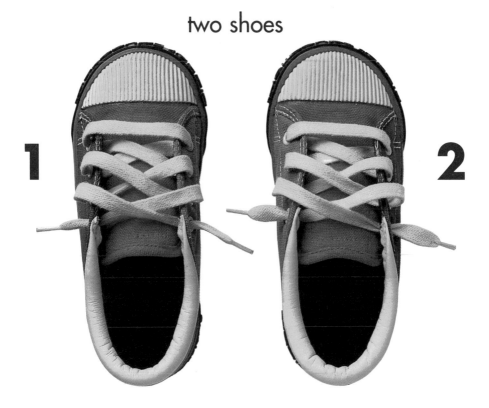

1   2

3
three

1

three bananas

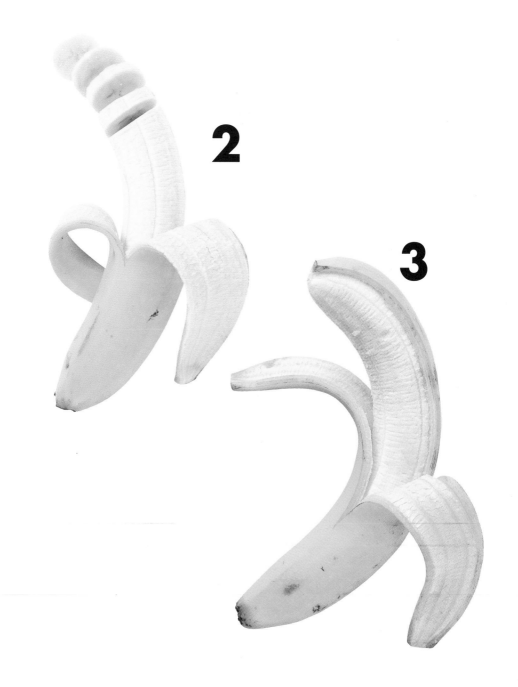

2

3

4
four

four pancakes

5
five

1

2

five kittens

3

4

5

6

six

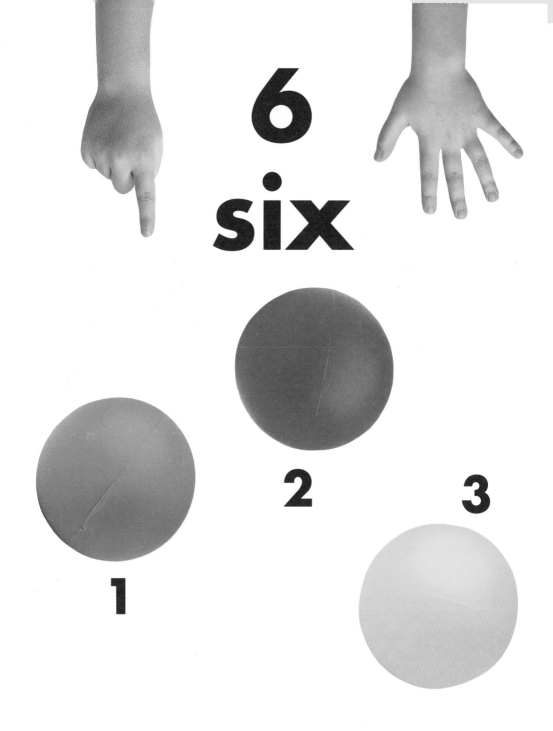

1

2

3

4

5

6

six balls

7

seven

seven flowers

8

eight

1 2 3

eight ducklings

9

nine

nine watermelon slices

1

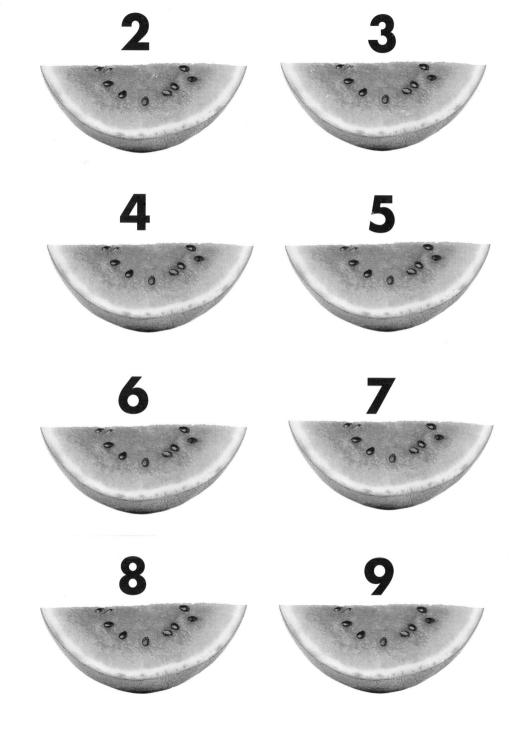

10
ten

1 **2** **3** **4**

ten teddy bears

5

6

7

8

9

10

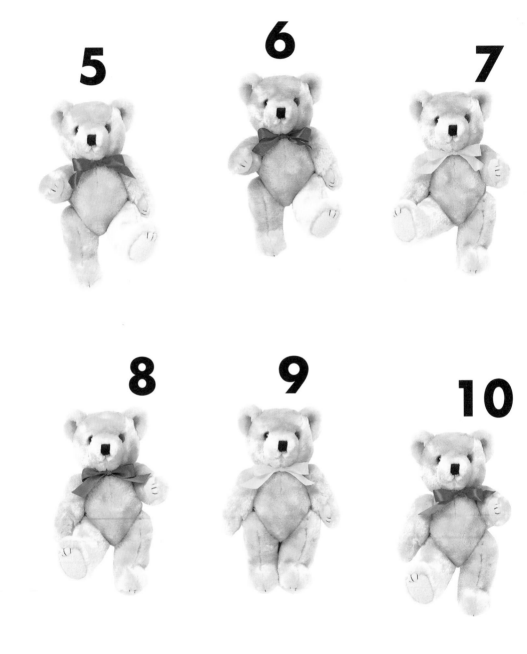